Tarot of the Soul

Copyright © 1995 by Belinda Atkinson. All rights reserved.
No part of this book may be reproduced in any form or by any electronic or mechanical means including information and retrieval systems without prior permissions from the publisher in writing.

Atkinson, Belinda, 1966-
    Tarot of the soul / Belinda Atkinson. -- 1st ed.
p. cm.

ISBN 0-926524-32-1: (alk. paper) $8.95
1. Tarot. 2. Self-management (Psychology)--Miscellanea. 3. Divination. I. Title.

BF1879.T2A85 1995   95-30170
133.3'2424--dc20   CIP

DESIGN IMPLEMENTATION: Carlene Lynch
COVER ART: Marcia Barrentine
AUTHOR PHOTO: Jack Germsheid

Printed in the United States of America.

Address all inquiries:
Wild Flower Press
P. O. Box 726
Newberg, OR 97132
U.S.A.

Printed on recycled paper.

YOUR SOUL IS WILLING AND ABLE TO ASSIST YOU IN ALL FACETS OF YOUR LIFE!

Synchronicities, intuitive thoughts and gut feelings are just a few ways in which your Soul helps you fulfill the needs of your incarnation and warns you when you get off track. Your Soul understands your strengths, your weaknesses, your needs for spiritual evolution and your requirements for happiness in this life.

With *Tarot of the Soul*, you use a regular deck of playing cards to access the knowledge and wisdom of your Soul. It is a thoughtful, positive, healing and motivational language. It reminds you of the beauty of life and the need to follow your heart.

Tarot of the Soul is the starting point of a trusting and evolving relationship with your Soul.

TAROT
of the SOUL

Belinda Atkinson

Swan•Raven & Co.
P. O. Box 726
Newberg, OR 97132

For Brenda --
My friend, my sister and my spiritual guide.

TABLE OF CONTENTS

Introduction	7
How Divination Works	9
Chapter 1	
Formulating Questions	12
Step-By-Step Guide to Drawing Cards	13
Tips on Reading Your Own Cards	15
Tips on Reading For Others	16
Chapter 2	
How Spreads Work	18
The Daily Arrow Spread	19
Four-Card Spread	20
Ten-Card Spread	21
The Magick Circle of Solomon	22
Circle of Destiny	23
Chart	24
Chapter 3	
Spades	25
Chapter 4	
Hearts	39
Chapter 5	
Diamonds	53
Chapter 6	
Clubs	67

INTRODUCTION

If someone could tell you what your life will be like a year from now or ten years from now, would you pursue the answer? It's a difficult question; one which requires a great deal of contemplation.

The idea that you can get a "sneak preview" into your future is a tough concept to grasp. You might first wonder if there is such a thing as destiny? If there isn't, then surely you will strive to change things you don't like about your future. Yet if you change certain aspects of your life, you may be cutting yourself off from important experiences and lessons. And if you alter your life, you may, quite possibly, create troubles more severe than the ones you are trying to shelter yourself from.

If there is such a thing as fate, and you receive bad news about the future, then you must live with the idea that something bad will happen before it occurs. It's hard enough to deal with problems as they arise, but to have foreknowledge of a painful event -- all the while having your hands tied behind your back -- would only serve to intensify and prolong the pain.

Why then is there such a thing as Divination? Why, throughout our history, have we wanted to know the future?

Astrology was practiced in Ancient Egypt, Greece, India, China and the Islamic world. The I Ching (which in modern times uses the tossing of coins) has been around for about 3,900 years.

If there wasn't a pressing need within the human psyche to want to know the future, we never would have developed so many methods of Divination. Here are 19 of the most common methods: In Palmistry the reader studies the hands. In Phrenology, the proportions of the head are read. In Botomancy, the leaves of plants are studied. In Crystallomancy, the reader gazes into a crystal ball. In Bibliomancy, one randomly flips to a page of the Bible. Sortilege involves the throwing of dice. Rhabdomancy studies the movements of a rod or stick held in the hand. Lithomancy is the study of patterns formed when pebbles are

tossed to the ground. Onomancy is the study of the letters in a person's name. Numerology uses important numbers in a person's life. Oneiromancy uses dreams to foretell events. And don't forget Automatic Writing, Ouija Boards, Seances, Psychometry (getting psychic impressions from a person's possessions), the studying of Auras, Table Tipping, Handwriting Analysis and, the most common these days, Cartomancy, the reading of Tarot or playing cards.

There must be a deep desire within the human animal to know what is yet to be. I believe the answer lies in the words "fortune telling." Instead of the terms "future telling" or "destiny telling," the more common word "fortune" implies an improved state of affairs: wealth, success, happiness, gain. People, I feel, aren't looking for fact so much as they are looking for hope of something better.

Early Cartomancy did not fill this need for hope. Instead, some Tarot methods scared listeners with talk of devastation, loss and death. They played on fears of the unknown with definitions such as "a dark-haired lady is jealous and will try to destroy you" and "bad news will come from overseas."

Yet Divination can just as easily steer us in more positive directions as it can warn us of impending doom.

It is a language, nothing more. Like the optimist versus the pessimist, it can focus on the positive aspects of our lives and lead us toward emotional strengthening or it can concern itself only with negatives and deflate our sense of hope and control.

I have endeavored to create a language that is motivational, healing and helpful. Rather than giving control to fate, the cards motivate the reader to strive for growth and improvement in areas where change is needed and acceptance in areas where change is not appropriate.

I hope you enjoy *Tarot of the Soul*. My most profound wish is that it serves as the starting point for a deeper and more immediate contact with the inner knowledge in your Soul.

HOW DIVINATION WORKS

How could an ordinary deck of cards possibly tell you something about yourself, your life and your future? After all, cards are just paper, ink and plastic. Nothing more.

Yet as you get to know *Tarot of the Soul* and become comfortable with the definitions of the cards, you'll discover there's something to it. Cards that start in your future will move to your present and then to your past, in rhythm with events that are taking place in your life.

There are dozens of explanations for this seeming miracle. Some think the Devil has his hand in the deck. Some think ghosts help us choose the cards that most suit our situation.

Just as anyone who has ever written a book on Divination, I too have my theory.

I believe each of us has a Soul which accompanies us in our many incarnations. I also believe that prior to each incarnation, we choose to learn certain lessons, overcome certain weaknesses, accomplish certain goals and, perhaps, right certain wrongs. I don't believe we choose every facet of our lives. Perhaps, before we are born, we give ourselves a general agenda or "To Do" list. How we tackle the items on our list is most likely a matter of trial and error.

As we're busy making a life for ourselves, I believe our Soul watches our progress and steps in to give us a little nudge when we get off track.

Often, these nudges come in the form of hunches or gut feelings. Have you ever left the house with the nagging feeling that you were forgetting something only to discover later that you had left an important item at home? Have you ever gotten a strong first impression about someone (whether negative or positive) only to discover later that your feelings were correct?

There are other ways the soul nudges you as well. Synchronicities are common. Seemingly unrelated events occur again and again. A word keeps popping up in conversation, you keep hearing a certain piece of music, or you keep encountering the same number.

During a three month period when I was looking for work and very confused over what career direction to take, I had the uncanny experience of only looking at the clock when it was 23 minutes after the hour. This went on sometimes five times a day for three long months. I don't believe the number 23 was significant. I think it was my Soul's way of comforting me. While at first the experience was alarming, after a while I felt as though someone or something was hearing my confusion and working toward a resolution.

I feel that the Soul is very willing to assist us in making good choices in our lives. I also believe that we can turn to our Souls to help us with our "To Do" lists. There are two things we have to do if we want to use the wisdom in our Souls to improve our lives: listen to the messages we receive and take action. Neither is easy. In order to listen we must first understand the messages. Unfortunately, it's sometimes very difficult to distinguish between our own outward wants and the inner advice we receive.

That's why I developed *Tarot of the Soul*. It's a simple language that you can use to contact your Soul and ask its advice. Whenever you are unsure of how to proceed in a situation, simply ask your Soul what is best. You will receive answers which help you understand your strengths and weaknesses.

To begin, turn to Chapter One. This section will explain how to formulate a question, how to read your own cards and how to read other people's cards. This section also provides tips which will help you to get more accurate readings. Next, choose a question and turn to Chapter Two to select an appropriate spread.

CHAPTER ONE

HOW TO READ THE CARDS

FORMULATING QUESTIONS

Tarot of the Soul focuses on your strengths and weaknesses. Rather than telling you that fate will determine the outcome of any given situation, the cards give you the opportunity to decide the best course of action based on your abilities, your needs for wholeness and the external factors influencing the situation.

It's important that you retain your decision-making power in the wording of your questions. Questions such as "Will I marry my high-school sweetheart and live happily ever after?" simply don't work. Marriages don't thrive because two people are meant to be together. A good relationship requires dedication, respect, a sense of humor and a lot of hard work.

You'll get a far better reading if you ask questions that help you to make improvements in your life: Do I have the emotional maturity required to commit to a long-term relationship? Do I have the strength needed to make it through any tough times that we may encounter? Am I entering this marriage for the right reasons? Are there any weaknesses that I should work on to improve our relationship? Will our family and friends be supportive of our marriage or will they be negative influences?

Here are a few general example questions which cover the emotional, physical, mental and spiritual areas of your life:

1. Do I have the emotional strength necessary to undertake and succeed in making this change in my life?
2. Will the external factors involved in this situation work for or against my success in reaching this goal?
3. Is there something that I am doing -- either consciously or subconsciously -- to impede my progress in this endeavour?
4. Is this endeavor in keeping with my needs for growth and spiritual evolution?

STEP-BY-STEP GUIDE TO DRAWING CARDS

You will develop your own style of reading the cards as you practice. In my case, I followed the instructions to the letter when I first began playing with I-Ching, Runes and various versions of the Tarot. Eventually, I dropped certain practices and adopted new ones which felt more comfortable for me.

If you're new to the whole area of Divination, I offer a simple step-by-step guide for you to follow. For additional tips on reading your own cards, please see page 15.

1. Find a quiet, comfortable place with a table large enough to spread the cards out.
2. Decide if you want to use one of the spreads outlined in Chapter Two or simply pull an undetermined number of cards in answer to your question.
3. Begin shuffling the entire, 52-card deck as you formulate a question in your mind. For assistance in formulating a question, read the previous page.
4. Keep the question in your mind as you continue to shuffle. You can say the question out loud, think about the issue in your mind or visualize various aspects of the question. Let your mind relax and don't pay attention to the fact that you are shuffling the cards. You'll find that you suddenly become consciously aware that you are shuffling. As soon as you do, stop shuffling and spread the cards out across your table in a fan shape with the numbers facing down.
5. Still thinking of the question, brush your hand over the row of cards. It doesn't matter if you hold your hand over the cards or bring your hand low enough to touch them.
6. You will sense an energy coming from some cards. Take the cards that you are drawn to, one by one, and place them on top of each other.

7. If you are not using a spread, continue drawing cards until you no longer sense energy coming from any of the cards. Trust your intuition to know when you have enough cards. Each of the cards will apply to your overall question, with no importance being placed on the order in which the cards were drawn.
8. If you are using a spread, continue drawing cards until you have the appropriate number. Then, place the last card you drew (the card now at the top of the pile) in the number one position. Place the second to last card you drew in the number two position. Continue until all the cards follow the pattern of your spread.
9. Look first at the suits that you have chosen. If you've drawn mostly Spades, your mental energy is at the forefront of the situation. A majority of Hearts signifies that your emotions, attitudes and feelings are most important. Mostly Diamonds means that the physical world (health, finances, work, home life and material possessions) is at the forefront. Clubs stand for spiritual matters. If your cards are equally split up between all the suits, this tells you the issue at hand effects all parts of your nature equally.
10. Now that you have done a brief assessment of the suits, you can begin reading the detailed descriptions of each card.
11. The reading seems to work best when you stop after each card and think about how the definition relates to the issue at hand. Don't be too concerned if a card doesn't always literally coincide with its placement in a spread. It's more important that you meditate on how the card applies to your overall question.
12. Once you've finished the entire reading, fill in the chart on page 24 (or a photocopy). Write down the date, the question and the cards you received. As time goes by, you will begin to see many interesting patterns emerge.

TIPS ON READING YOUR OWN CARDS

1. Make sure you are relaxed and focused on your question before you select your cards. If you are in a hurry, if you have a lot on your mind, or if your thoughts are competing with noise, you won't get an accurate reading.
2. Rituals can be used to assist you in easily falling into a receptive and relaxed state of mind. A few examples might be playing a favorite piece of music and lighting a candle every time you sit down to read your cards.
3. Don't ask an emotionally charged question unless you are prepared to hear the truth. Often, I've asked questions hoping for a positive response and received a negative answer which I was not ready to accept.
4. *Never* use the advice you receive from the cards as your sole reason for making changes in your life. The cards are only meant to assist you. Use your experience, intuition, spiritual beliefs, morals and your understanding of the external factors involved as your primary guides.
5. Don't draw a new card just because you don't like the answer you receive. If you do, it is very possible that you will receive the same card you just got rid of.
6. Once you are comfortable with the cards and their meanings, try experimenting with the cards and developing your own spreads. This is an excellent way to develop a deeper rapport with the cards.
7. Buy your own deck of cards specifically for the purpose of reading. If you like, you can write an overview of each definition on your cards. It speeds up the reading process and enables you to more easily see the relationships between the many ideas being expressed in your readings.

TIPS ON READING FOR OTHERS

1. Never try to talk someone into having their cards read. If they are apprehensive or nervous, respect their feelings. They will come to you if and when they want an outside view.
2. Don't read anyone else's cards until you've practiced and feel comfortable with the meanings of the cards and the results of your own readings.
3. Preface a card reading by assuring the person that the cards will merely provide an overview of their strengths and weaknesses in any given situation. They should trust their own instincts, experience, morals and the external factors involved in any given situation over and above anything the cards have to say.
4. You don't need to know the question that is being asked in order to give a reading.
5. Explore your intuition in readings. Many people who are attracted to Divination and Cartomancy possess well developed psychic skills. If you are reading a friend's cards and feel the urge to share a thought of your own on the subject, do so. It will be best, however, to clarify what part of the reading is from the book and what part is your own perception.
6. If you have a serious interest in Cartomancy, do additional research. There are many books on the market, both good and bad, which teach you how to see and understand other people's auras and conduct psychometry (picking up vibrations from objects). These can be useful additions to a card reading.

CHAPTER TWO

SPREADS

HOW SPREADS WORK

Those who are new to Cartomancy may wonder why it's necessary to use spreads. It is not necessary, at least not with *Tarot of the Soul*. If you prefer, you can follow the basic directions outlined on page 13 and pull as many cards as you are drawn towards. Each of the cards will give you insight into your overall question. The only difference is that you don't assign any particular importance to the placement of the cards.

The spreads are here to help you focus on the many different aspects of your questions so you can more easily reach a decision. They work much like the human mind works in this regard.

Suppose, for example, you are grappling with the age-old question about what to cook for dinner. The easiest way to solve this dilemma is to break the question down into a number of smaller questions, such as: What supplies do I have on hand? Do I have the time and inclination to go to the grocery store to pick up more supplies? How hungry am I? Am I in the mood for something rich and high in calories or something light and nutritious? Do I have time to cook something special or should I make something fast so I can eat right away?

The spreads presented here will help you to see the many factors involved in your questions. However, it's important that you don't get frustrated if the definition of a card doesn't literally coincide with its placement. You won't always see an obvious correlation, particularly in the larger spreads such as The Magick Circle of Solomon and the Ten-Card Spread.

If, after some consideration, you can't see any way in which a card fits in with its placement, meditate instead on how the card fits in with the overall question.

It may take some practice and patience, but if you keep an open mind and strive to see the spreads in metaphorical rather than literal terms, you will gain insight into your questions and yourself.

THE DAILY ARROW

Here is a simple spread that can be performed on a regular basis (once a day, once a week, once a month, once a year) or when the mood arises.

The spread presents a general overview of the current situation, the action which should be taken and the new situation which will evolve once the action is completed.

It's a great spread for straight-forward questions, but it's somewhat brief for issues of major importance in your life.

Remember:
♠ = Mental Energy
♥ = Emotional Energy
♦ = Physical Energy
♣ = Spiritual Energy

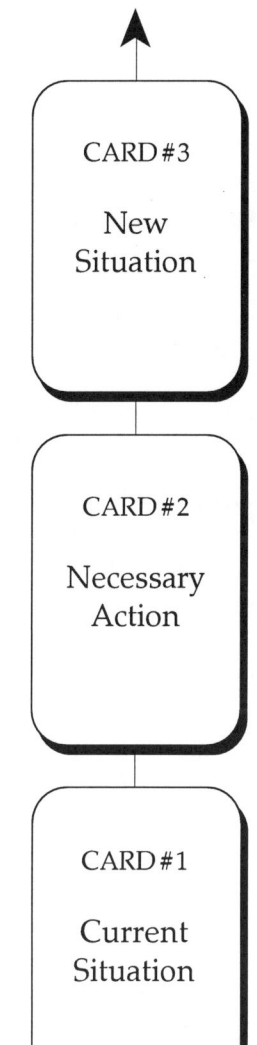

FOUR-CARD SPREAD

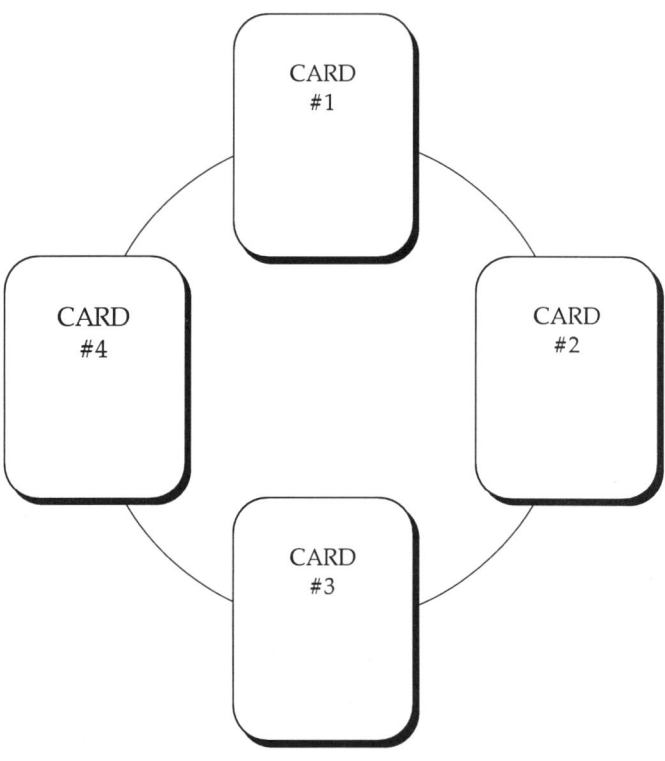

Card 1: The current situation.

Card 2: The sacrifice which may be required to bring about change for the better.

Card 3: The potential rewards that are available to you now.

Card 4: The future of the situation if events continue on their present path.

Remember: ♠ = Mental Energy ♥ = Emotional Energy
♦ = Physical Energy ♣ = Spiritual Energy

TEN-CARD SPREAD

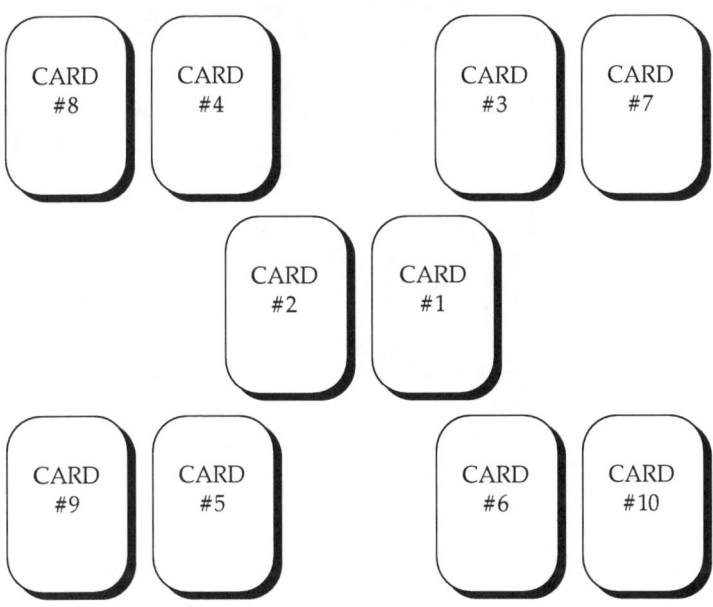

Cards 1 & 2:   The essence of the question and the questioner.

Cards 3 & 7:   The natural direction in which the situation will progress.

Cards 4 & 8:   The direction in which the situation will progress if forced. If Cards 3, 7, 4 and 8 are compatible, the situation will progress in the same direction whether you let things unfold naturally or try to force change. If the cards contradict one another, the situation will change depending on your actions.

Cards 9 & 5:   How your mental and spiritual energy is impacting the situation.

Cards 6 & 10: The future of the situation if events progress on the current path.

Remember: ♠ = Mental Energy   ♥ = Emotional Energy
♦ = Physical Energy   ♣ = Spiritual Energy

THE MAGICK CIRCLE OF SOLOMON

(Ancient 10-Card Spread)

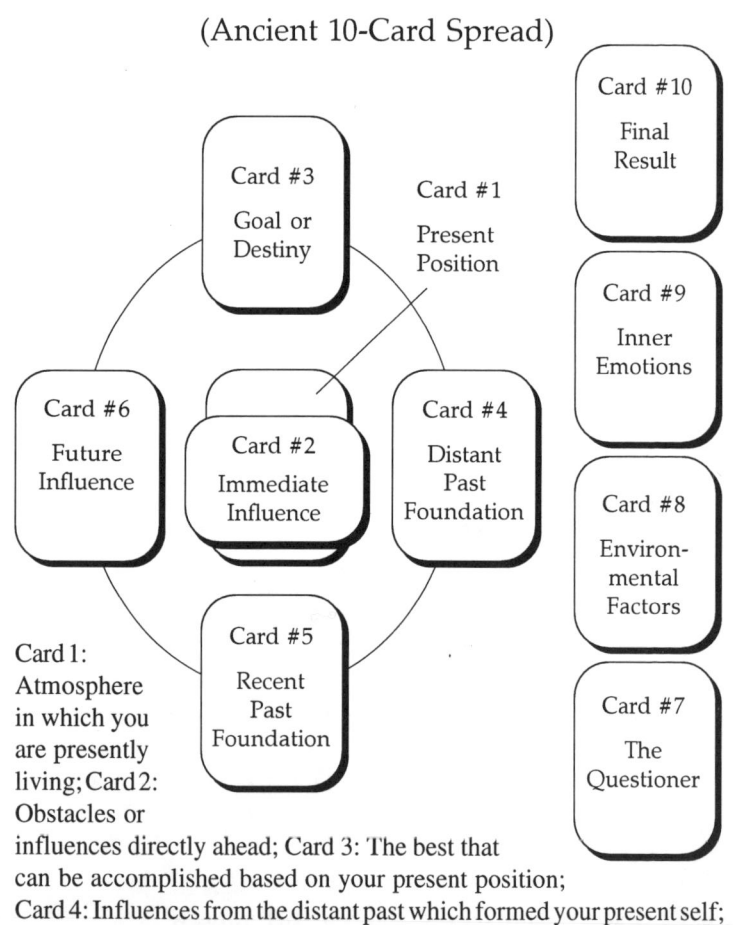

Card 1: Atmosphere in which you are presently living; Card 2: Obstacles or influences directly ahead; Card 3: The best that can be accomplished based on your present position; Card 4: Influences from the distant past which formed your present self; Card 5: Events which are now passing or recently passed; Card 6: Events in near future; Card 7: Your present attitude; Card 8: Your influence on others and their influence on you; Card 9: Your inner hopes, fears and anxieties; Card 10: The final result.

Remember: ♠ = Mental Energy ♥ = Emotional Energy
♦ = Physical Energy ♣ = Spiritual Energy

CIRCLE OF DESTINY

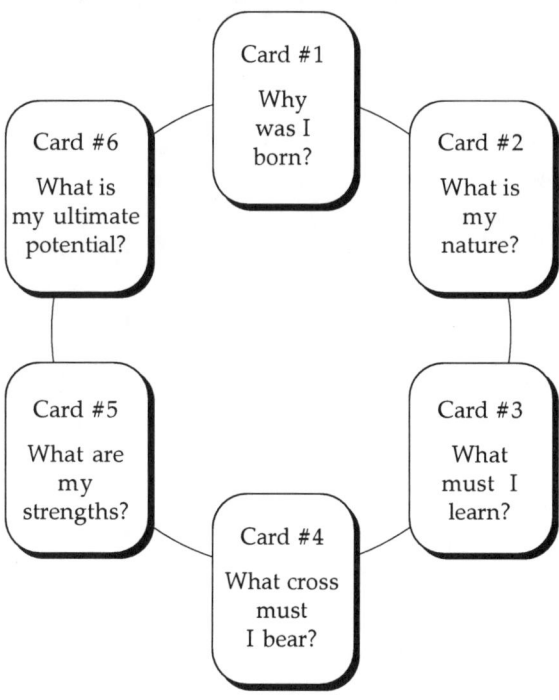

This spread should not be done too often. It focuses on your agenda in this incarnation or your "To Do" list as I described in the section "How Divination Works."

Card 1: Your mandate (what you are here to accomplish).
Card 2: What brings you wholeness and happiness from the deepest core of who you are.
Card 3: The lessons you must learn in this incarnation.
Card 4: The adversities and shortcomings you were born to overcome or accept as a part of yourself.
Card 5: The blessings you were given in this incarnation.
Card 6: Your greatest potential for success and happiness.

Remember: ♠ = Mental Energy   ♥ = Emotional Energy
♦ = Physical Energy   ♣ = Spiritual Energy

DATE	QUESTION	CARDS RECEIVED

CHAPTER THREE

SPADES

Spades are concerned with mental energy.
When you pull a Spade from the deck,
you have the opportunity to gain wisdom,
insight and a strengthened
sense of self worth.

ACE OF SPADES

INTUITION

This card represents a failure to draw upon your own Inner Voice or Intuition in some regard. You are turning outward for answers to your questions when deep down inside, you already know the correct path to take.

Your Inner Voice is not concerned with finding the easiest path or the least painful road. Sometimes movement forward involves discomfort and pain. And often, what you perceive as a treacherous road may be the only route leading to success.

Rather than consulting friends and family in hopes they will suggest less complicated action, trust and follow your Intuition.

This is the only voice that can see the results of all the alternatives currently presenting themselves. This is the only voice that knows your deepest needs for growth and fulfilment.

Now more than ever, your Intuition is available for use in decision making.

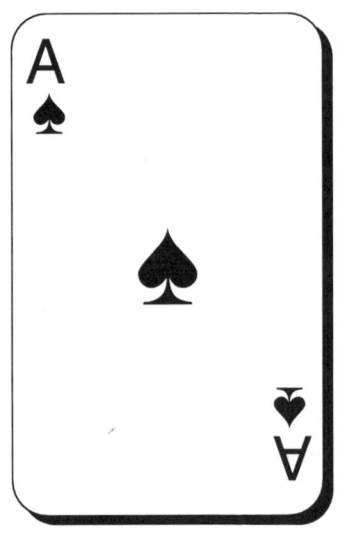

QUICK REFERENCE:
This card represents a failure to draw upon your own Intuition in some regard. You are turning to friends and family for advice when deep down inside you already know the correct path to take. Trust and follow your Intuition. It will lead you to success.

TWO OF SPADES

NEGATIVE THINKING

You now have the strength and opportunity to release negative thought patterns.

Rather than fearing that things won't work out or preparing for the worst, erase these thought patterns and start assuming and preparing for success.

If you tell yourself often enough that you will fail or that things won't work out, your subconscious mind will find a way to make your thoughts a reality. If, however, you continually tell yourself that your efforts are bearing fruit, your subconscious mind will work toward these goals.

You've no doubt dreaded attending an event and suddenly found yourself battling a cold or flu. This is one small example of your subconscious mind outwardly responding to your inner thoughts.

Your subconscious hears each and every thought. Make a conscious effort to ensure you are using your subconscious mind in productive and positive ways.

QUICK REFERENCE:
This is a great time to release negative thought patterns. Rather than fearing that things won't work out or preparing yourself for the worst, work to push your mind in more positive directions. Tell yourself that things are working out and you are succeeding. Your subconscious mind will find a way of making your thoughts a reality.

THREE OF SPADES

UNDERESTIMATING

You now have the opportunity to release patterns of underestimating yourself and your abilities.

No one on this earth is perfect. We all have weaknesses, faults and bad habits. Each of us is well suited to contribute to society in some ways while ill suited in others.

If you can recognize your weaknesses as a natural and appropriate part of who you are, your sense of worth does not suffer.

If, however, you believe your weaknesses make you less valuable or less able to contribute, then you underestimate your worth and do harm to yourself.

Recognize the many ways you enrich other people's lives. Like the pebble that creates a great ripple in the river, your acts of kindness and your special talents find their way into many people's hearts and lives.

You are valuable.

Strive to appreciate your strengths and accept your weaknesses.

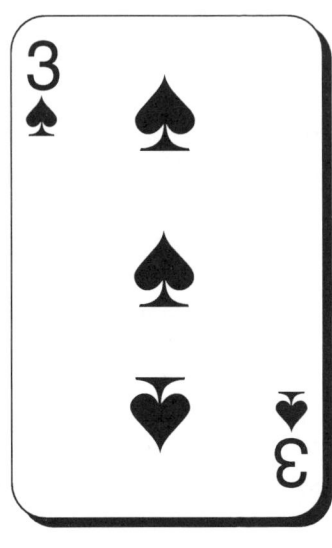

QUICK REFERENCE:
You now have the opportunity to release patterns of underestimating yourself. None of us is perfect. We all have strengths in certain areas and weaknesses in others. If you believe your weaknesses make you less valuable, then you underestimate your worth and do harm to yourself. Recognize the many ways you improve other people's lives.

FOUR OF SPADES

COMPARISONS

You now have the opportunity and strength to stop comparing yourself with other people and your life with the lives of others.

There will always be people who are better off than you just as there will always be people who are less fortunate.

Each of us is on our own unique journey. Each one of us has gifts, talents and blessings to enjoy as well as burdens, setbacks and disappointments to bear.

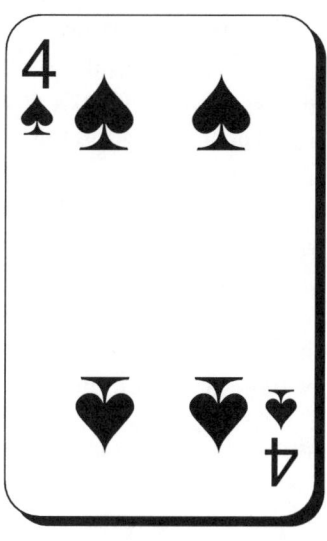

What you see as a blessing in someone else's life may, in actuality, be a burden. And what you see as a burden in your life may be a wonderful opportunity to gain strength, wisdom and spiritual evolution.

Resist the urge to compare yourself with others and focus on your own requirements for growth.

When you celebrate your blessings and accept your burdens, you are rewarded with a deeper understanding of what you can contribute to society in this incarnation.

QUICK REFERENCE:
You now have the opportunity to stop comparing yourself with other people and your life with other people's lives. There will always be those who are more fortunate than you just as there will always be those who are less fortunate. Each one of us is on our own, unique journey. Each one of us has blessings to enjoy and burdens to bear. Resist the urge to compare and focus on your own requirements for growth.

FIVE OF SPADES

INVENTORY

You now have the insight necessary to undertake a personal inventory. Each one of us is continually growing and changing. Our goals and requirements for wholeness shift as we face new challenges.

We need to stop every once in a while and conduct an inventory to ensure our actions are in keeping with our needs for happiness and wholeness.

Take time to ensure you are working toward goals which are in keeping with your needs. Ask yourself whether or not your occupation, relationships and hobbies are enriching your life or preventing you from spending time on endeavours and activities which would bring you more in alignment with your nature. Look at your strengths and weaknesses; think about the areas in which you would like to improve.

Once you have a clear understanding of what you need for wholeness, you can begin removing resistances and creating a life which is more in alignment with who you are.

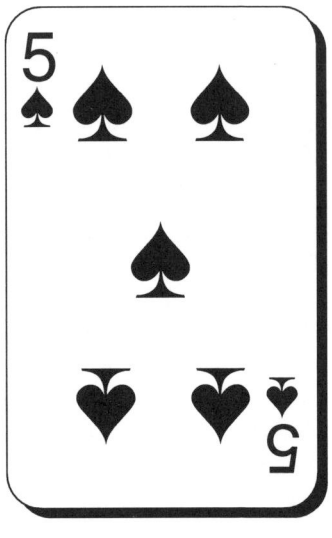

QUICK REFERENCE:
You now have the insight necessary to take an inventory of yourself and your life. Each one of us is continually growing and changing. Our goals and our requirements for wholeness are continually shifting as we face new challenges. We need to stop every once in a while and conduct an inventory to ensure our actions are in keeping with our needs for happiness and wholeness. Make sure you are working toward goals which are in keeping with your needs for happiness and wholeness.

SIX OF SPADES

GENERALIZATIONS

As soon as we can understand simple language, we begin receiving signals about who we are. We learn in subtle and obvious ways about our strengths and weaknesses. Family, friends and teachers tell us we are shy or outgoing, creative or logical, funny or serious, leaders or followers, lazy or hard working, smart or dumb.

At best, these remarks help us pursue development in areas where we have natural gifts and talents. At worst, they limit our understanding of ourselves.

This card is asking if there are any ways in which you limit your understanding of yourself based on old or outmoded generalizations.

If you believe, for example, that you are a follower, ask if you've allowed yourself an opportunity to lead.

It does not matter whether you succeed or fail. What's important is the satisfaction that comes from overcoming apprehension and taking on new challenges.

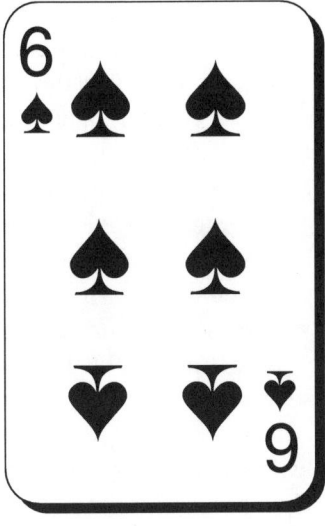

QUICK REFERENCE:
As soon as we can understand language, we begin receiving signals about who we are. Parents, teachers and friends tell us we are shy or outgoing, creative or logical, funny or serious, leaders or followers, lazy or hard working, smart or dumb. This card is asking if there are any ways in which you limit your understanding of yourself based on old or outmoded generalizations.

SEVEN OF SPADES

NO LUCK

If you are striving to move forward in some situation, this card is a gentle reminder that luck will have no effect on the outcome. You will succeed if you have the right attitude, work hard, act in a timely manner and if the outcome is in keeping with your needs for growth.

Sometimes we chalk up our successes and failures to luck, either good or bad. But good luck will not bring you success if you haven't done the work required for growth. And bad luck will not make you fail if you have done everything necessary to bring about success.

If you want success, be prepared to undertake the work and don't let luck, fate, superstition, fear of failure or fear of success stand in your way.

This card also invites you to re-examine a past failure which was dismissed as bad luck. Search for meaning. With every failure comes an opportunity to grow. Learn all you can from past failures and you won't have to repeat them in order to grow.

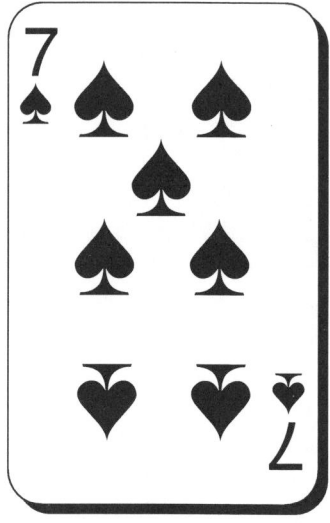

QUICK REFERENCE:
If you are striving to move forward in some situation, endeavour or relationship, this card is a reminder that luck will have no effect on the outcome. Good luck cannot make you succeed if you haven't done the work required for growth. And bad luck will not make you fail if you have done everything necessary to bring about success. This card also invites you to re-examine a past failure which was dismissed as bad luck. Learn all you can from your failures and you won't have to repeat them in order to grow.

EIGHT OF SPADES

NEW LIFE

Each one of us would do certain things differently if we could begin our lives again. Some would change a few minor details, while others would completely re-write their personal histories.

This card is asking you a simple question: Why can't you begin again?

If you want something badly enough, and if you're prepared to work for it and make the necessary sacrifices, you can make any change in your life.

If you've always dreamed of pursuing a hobby, occupation or interest, but did not, ask yourself why.

Is the dream unattainable or do you hesitate because you feel the opportunity has passed you by? Rather than staying on a present course because you feel you have no alternative, understand you are always free to begin again.

Before you proceed, however, ensure your expectations are realistic and not the result of an active and optimistic imagination.

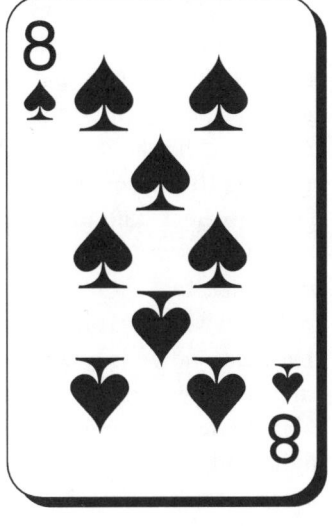

QUICK REFERENCE:
Each one of us would do certain things differently if we could begin our lives again.
Some would make small changes, while others would completely re-write their personal histories. This card is asking a simple question: Why can't you begin again? If you want something badly enough, if you are prepared to undertake the work and make . the necessary sacrifices, you can succeed in making any change in your life. Before you proceed, however, ensure your expectations are realistic.

NINE OF SPADES

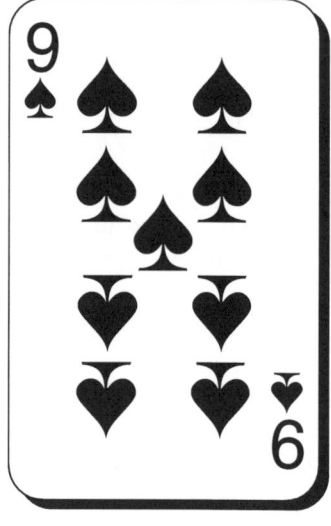

SEEKING WISDOM

Can you spot the wise man at a gathering? Is he the one going on at length about his ideas or is he the one quietly listening to the conversation? The wise man knows he can learn nothing from hearing his own voice.

The wise man recognizes that each one of us -- whether king or beggar, thief or judge -- has knowledge, wisdom, insight and experience that is worth hearing and exploring.

If we fail to listen, or if we refuse to open our minds to other people's ideas, then, like the fool who loves to hear his own voice, we miss the opportunity to gain knowledge and insight.

This card is asking you to pay particular attention to other people's ideas. Even a chance meeting with a stranger can bring wisdom. Even a naive child can offer insight.

When you maintain an open, non-judgmental mind and a listening ear, you can benefit from every Soul you encounter.

QUICK REFERENCE:
Can you spot the wise man at a gathering? Is he the one going on at length about his ideas or is he the one quietly listening to the conversation? The wise man knows he can learn nothing from hearing his own voice. He recognizes that each one of us -- whether king or beggar, thief or judge -- has knowledge, wisdom, experience and insight that is worth hearing and exploring. When you maintain an open, non-judgemental mind and a listening ear, you can benefit from every Soul you encounter.

TEN OF SPADES

RE-PROGRAMMING

The Ten of Spades asks you to think positively about some situation or relationship which is causing you anxiety. Rather than fearing failure or preparing for the worst, program your subconscious mind for success.

As you set the ground work toward your goals in your external actions, keep telling your subconscious mind that you are making progress and succeeding.

When fears and doubts arise, rather than giving these thoughts power and control, persistently work to turn your thoughts in more positive directions. This can work in all facets of your life. If, for example, you feel physically ill, tell your subconscious mind over and over that you feel well.

Regardless of your goals (whether involving work, relationships, health, finances, spiritual growth, emotional fulfillment or breaking a habit), you can move in more positive directions with conscious effort and subconscious re-programming.

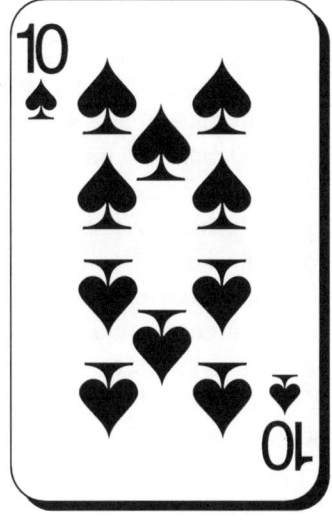

QUICK REFERENCE:
Think positively about some situation or relationship which is causing you anxiety. Re-program your subconscious mind for success. When fears and doubts arise, rather than giving these thoughts power and control, persistently work to turn the thoughts in more positive directions. This re-programming can work in all facets of your life.

JACK OF SPADES

RELEASE

If you are unclear about how to proceed in a situation or relationship, release the dilemma to your subconscious mind.

Rather than fretting over the decision, ask your subconscious mind to take control.

Release it, forget it and resist the urge to let it filter back into your conscious thoughts. Your answer will come to you soon enough.

Your subconscious mind has great potential to improve your life. Stored within is every lesson you've learned and every feeling you've felt.

More importantly, your subconscious mind is the essence of your Soul. It understands why you were put on this earth and what you are here to learn.

When you release a problem to your subconscious mind, you receive an answer based on your needs for growth.

You may not always like the answer your subconscious mind provides, but try to remember you are getting advice based on your most profound requirements for growth.

QUICK REFERENCE:
If you are unclear how to proceed in a certain situation or relationship, release the dilemma to your subconscious mind. Rather than fretting over the decision, ask your subconscious mind to take control. Release it, forget it and resist the urge to let the dilemma filter back into your conscious mind. Your answer will come to you soon enough.

QUEEN OF SPADES

UNDERSTANDING

Each of us faces struggles, setbacks and difficulties in our lives. Occasionally, we are presented with obstacles of such a profound nature, that they ultimately change the way in which we live and our understanding of the world.

You have recently overcome a hardship in your life. It may have been a profound obstacle which altered your world or it may have been a smaller event which carried less significant consequences. Regardless of the magnitude, you are now required to find meaning.

None of us is given a struggle without also being given an opportunity to learn and grow. What did you learn? Did you gain insight into your needs for happiness? Did you become a stronger person? Did you become closer to someone in your life?

Seek to discover every way in which you've benefited as a result of your recent struggles and try to incorporate this insight and understanding into all facets of your life.

QUICK REFERENCE:
You've recently overcome a challenge, setback or struggle in your life. It may have been a profound obstacle which deeply affected your understanding of your life or it may have been a smaller, less significant event. Now is the time to find understanding. Discover every way in which you've grown from this event and incorporate this new-found knowledge and understanding into all facets of your life.

KING OF SPADES

INSPIRATION

From time to time, we are granted fleeting, yet extraordinary, moments of truth and understanding.

Sometimes referred to as ecstasy or reverie, it's a sensation of being outside oneself and seeing the entire world with new eyes. It's a feeling of crystal clarity and seemingly boundless insight into ourselves and our place in the world.

You now have the ability to attain this kind of inspiration.

Seek out every opportunity to remove yourself from the noise and confusion of life.

Find the places and circumstances which bring you peace and serenity, and listen to the wisdom that comes when your external world is settled and your mind is open for internal exploration.

The insight you receive is your Soul urging you to make important and lasting changes in your life.

Act on the wisdom of your Soul and you will be blessed with growth, fulfilment and spiritual evolution.

QUICK REFERENCE:
You have the heightened ability to experience moments of Inspiration. Sometimes referred to as ecstasy or reverie, it's a feeling of crystal clarity and seemingly boundless insight into yourself and your place in the world. This is your Soul urging you to make important and lasting changes in your life.

CHAPTER FOUR

HEARTS

♥

Hearts are concerned with emotions,
attitudes and feelings. When you pull a
Heart from the deck, there is an opportunity
to gain a greater sense of happiness
and wholeness.

♥

ACE OF HEARTS

ANGER

The Ace of Hearts is concerned with releasing feelings of anger which are preventing advancement in some part of your emotional life.

It may be anger that is connected with an event from your past or it may be a response to circumstances which are now unfolding in your life. Regardless of the origin, it's integral to your emotional well-being and spiritual evolution that you work through these feelings.

In order to deal with anger effectively, it's important to acknowledge its power, understand how it affects your life, constructively confront the source of the anger, release the pain and, most important of all, forgive. It is never appropriate to hold anger inside.

Anger is a valid response to inappropriate behaviour, but those who hold on to anger continue to victimize themselves long after the event has run its course.

Refuse to let anger interfere with the many blessings that lay ahead.

QUICK REFERENCE:
The Ace of Hearts is concerned with feelings of anger which are preventing advancement in some part of your emotional life. In order to deal with anger effectively, it's important to acknowledge its power, understand how it affects your life, constructively confront the source of your anger, release the pain, and, most important of all, forgive. Those who hold on to anger continue to victimize themselves long after the event has run its course.

TWO OF HEARTS

FEAR

The Two of Hearts is concerned with releasing feelings of fear which are preventing you from moving forward in some aspect of your life.

Everyone experiences feelings of fear when they move in new directions. Everyone feels apprehension at the thought of moving beyond activities which are safe, familiar and predictable.

Those who work past fear are rewarded with a wonderful sense of accomplishment and satisfaction.

Those who are held back by fear miss out on the opportunities and challenges which are closest to their hearts. They are left only with feelings of regret over what might have been.

If there is a challenge, activity or goal which is particularly meaningful and heartfelt to you, allow yourself to explore the possibilities.

Remove yourself from the safe and predictable. Immerse yourself in the excitement of working toward your most profound desires.

QUICK REFERENCE:
The Two of Hearts is concerned with releasing feelings of fear which are preventing you from moving forward in some aspect of your life. Everyone experiences fear when they move in new directions. Don't let fear prevent you from exploring challenges, activities and goals which are particularly meaningful and heartfelt for you.

THREE OF HEARTS

GUILT

The Three of Hearts is concerned with releasing feelings of guilt which are preventing you from moving forward.

Regardless of how disconnected it may seem, guilt -- going as far back as childhood -- can affect your present life in many ways.

Guilt can remain in the conscious mind, effecting your sense of self worth and draining your emotional strength.

Guilt can also lurk in the dark corners of your subconscious, slowly taking away your ability to move forward and create new worlds for yourself.

If in the past you did or said something to cause pain to others, or committed an act which brings shame to your heart, it is integral to your emotional well-being that you forgive yourself.

You cannot change the past, but you can change the future. Accept that you are fallible, forgive yourself, and release the guilt that you have been using to punish yourself for past mistakes.

QUICK REFERENCE:
The Three of Hearts is concerned with releasing feelings of guilt which are preventing you from moving forward. Guilt can effect your life in many ways. If you have done or said something to cause pain to others, or committed an act which brings shame to your heart, it is time to forgive yourself and release the guilt that you have been using to punish yourself.

FOUR OF HEARTS

BITTERNESS

The Four of Hearts is concerned with releasing feelings of bitterness which are preventing you from creating new worlds for yourself.

Bitterness is a state of continually re-living the pain associated with an unfortunate circumstance. It is a state in which strength, energy and enthusiasm are consumed by resentment and suffering.

Don't suffer over your suffering. Rather than re-living the pain associated with an injustice, see it as a door leading to a new opportunity -- a challenge offering strengthening, insight and spiritual evolution.

Life's lessons come in all forms. Some are positive and inspiring, while others bring us pain and limitation. Yet every experience is an opportunity for growth.

If you can recognize pain and injustice as an opportunity to grow, you will quickly move forward.

Try to remember that some of the roughest roads lead to the most peaceful destinations.

QUICK REFERENCE:
The Four of Hearts is concerned with releasing feelings of bitterness which are preventing you from creating new worlds for yourself. Rather than continually re-living the pain associated with an injustice from the past, see it as a door leading to a new opportunity -- a challenge offering strengthening, insight and spiritual evolution. Try to remember that some of the roughest roads lead to the most peaceful destinations.

FIVE OF HEARTS

UNHAPPINESS

The Five of Hearts is concerned with feelings of unhappiness which are affecting your life in some way.

If you are experiencing unhappiness in some part of your life, seek to discover what brought this condition into effect.

Try to understand what you are holding on to that is creating unhappiness and what is required to steer your life in more positive directions.

Try to remember that unhappiness is often a gateway to more fortunate circumstances. Unhappiness serves to remind you that some aspect of the life you have been living is no longer appropriate to the person you have become.

Unhappiness is a signal that you are ready to grow and take on new challenges.

Rather than holding on to inappropriate circumstances and feeling unhappy, work to create a new world which is more in alignment with your requirements for happiness and wholeness.

QUICK REFERENCE:
The Five of Hearts is concerned with releasing feelings of unhappiness which are effecting your life in some way. Seek to discover what brought this condition into effect and understand what is required to steer your mind in more positive directions. Try to remember that unhappiness is oftcn a signal that the life you have been living is no longer appropriate to the person you have become. You are ready to grow and take on new challenges.

SIX OF HEARTS

PAUSE

We sometimes become so caught up in the mundane responsibilities of living -- bills, groceries, chores, deadlines -- we fail to recognize that life is a precious gift.

This card is urging you to contemplate the many gifts and blessings in your life. Health, friends, family, shelter, food, work, freedom...all are privileges that are sometimes ignored as rights.

Don't wait until you feel ill to understand the comfort of feeling well. Don't wait until a loved one is gone to recognize how much they added to your life. Don't wait until money is tight to understand the security of having fresh food on your table.

Pause and enjoy the many blessings in your life. Attempt to see, smell, touch and taste everything around you as if you are encountering it for the first time. And the next time you feel sad, lonely or unfulfilled in any aspect of your life, think of all the small privileges you enjoy every day.

QUICK REFERENCE:
Take time out from the mundane responsibilities of life -- bills, chores, deadlines -- to enjoy the many small privileges that are sometimes ignored as rights. Don't wait until you feel ill to understand the comfort of feeling well; don't wait until an argument with a loved one to recognize how much they add to your life. The next time you feel unhappy or unfulfilled, think of the small privileges you enjoy every day.

SEVEN OF HEARTS

ACCEPTANCE

The Seven of Hearts signifies a new-found sense of acceptance in some aspect of your emotional life.

You find you can more easily accept your shortcomings and more easily accept the beliefs, attitudes and shortcomings of others.

With acceptance comes the understanding that each of us is on our own separate journey. Each one of us has strengths and weaknesses which are integral to reaching our own destination.

Rather than feeling ashamed of your own weaknesses, you can more easily accept them as an appropriate part of who you are. Rather than feeling angry over other people's shortcomings (or beliefs and ideals which you do not share), you can more easily find acceptance

Now more than ever, you understand that persuading others to live by your beliefs is pointless; just as others have no right to force you to live according to their morals and ideals.

QUICK REFERENCE:
The Seven of Hearts signifies a new-found sense of acceptance in some aspect of your emotional life. You find you can more easily accept your shortcomings and more easily accept the beliefs, attitudes and shortcomings of others. With acceptance comes the understanding that each of us is on our own separate journey. Each one of us has strengths and weaknesses which are integral to reaching our own destination.

EIGHT OF HEARTS

JOY

The Eight of Hearts is a wonderful card, signifying a new-found sense of joy.

Rather than fretting over things that have happened in the past or worrying about events which may or may not unfold in the future, you are able to focus on the present and find joy in the daily act of working toward your goals.

Use this time to fully immerse yourself in the experience of living. Strive to notice the many small blessings that you might otherwise take for granted.

Create circumstances which bring you closest to the people and places that are most important to you.

Also, strive to share your new-found sense of joy with those close to you.

If you find that others cannot share your enthusiasm, remind them of the precarious nature of life.

Let them know that joy is only available when our hearts, minds, spirits and bodies are focused on the present.

QUICK REFERENCE:
The Eight of Hearts is a wonderful card, signifying a new-found sense of joy. Rather than fretting over things that have happened in the past or worrying about events which may or may not occur in the future, you are able to focus on the present and find joy in the many blessings of life.

NINE OF HEARTS

FAITH

The Nine of Hearts is a gentle reminder to have faith.

If you are uncertain how to feel about events which are now taking shape in your life, have faith that what is happening is appropriate to your advancement.

There is no way to fully understand life's journey. Often you travel blindly, not knowing the significance of the many turns and detours; not comprehending the importance of the many people you meet along the way.

In the end, you discover that every part of the journey was integral to reaching your destination.

Have faith that all parts of your journey -- the obstacles, setbacks and disappointments, as well as the joy, rewards and advancements -- bring you closer to spiritual evolution.

When you have faith, you can accept and overcome any challenge. When you have faith, you have the wisdom to see that every turn in the road is an opportunity and a blessing.

QUICK REFERENCE:
The Nine of Hearts is a gentle reminder to have faith. If you are uncertain about events which are now unfolding in your emotional life, have faith that what is happening is appropriate to your advancement.

TEN OF HEARTS

WILL

You can have success in almost any endeavor you take on at this time if you have the will to succeed.

You may have to make personal sacrifices and fight doubts from yourself and others. You may encounter difficulty as you move closer to your goal. At times, you may even become convinced that the final result is not worth the trouble.

But if you maintain your will, recognize doubt as a natural part of moving in new directions, and continue to undertake all the work involved, you will reap the rewards.

Remember, success is as much a product of will as it is a product of action. If, in your external actions, you strive to reach a goal that is not important in your heart, your subconscious mind will not assist you in reaching your goal.

If, however, you combine a strong will and a deep internal desire to succeed, then no setback, frustration or failure will stop you from eventually reaching your goals.

QUICK REFERENCE:
You can be successful in reaching your goals provided you have the will to succeed. You may have to make personal sacrifices and fight doubts from yourself and others. You may even become convinced that the result is not worth the trouble. But if you maintain your will, recognize doubts as a natural part of moving in new directions and continue to undertake the work, you will know success.

JACK OF HEARTS

PASSION

The Jack of Hearts is the passion card, signifying the need to seek out goals, desires, beliefs and interests which bring you passion.

Each one of us is passionate about certain things. Some are passionate about hobbies and interests. Some are passionate about political views. Some are passionate about spiritual or intellectual advancement. Some are passionate about professional goals.

Regardless of your passion, the Jack of Hearts is a reminder to honor those things which are most important to you.

Make sure that you are working toward those beliefs, goals, ideals and pursuits which are most heartfelt for you. Don't waste your valuable time and energy striving for goals which are not important.

So many people talk about the things they would like to do and the places they would like to see "someday." Unless you dedicate yourself to your passions, someday may never come.

QUICK REFERENCE:
The Jack of Hearts is the passion card, signifying the need to honor the goals, desires, beliefs and interests which bring you passion. Make sure that you are working toward your passions and not wasting your time and energy on goals which are not important. So many people talk about the things they would like to do and the places they would like to see "someday." Unless you dedicate yourself to your passions, someday may never come.

QUEEN OF HEARTS

UNCONDITIONAL LOVE

You now have the opportunity to give and receive unconditional love.

If you have worried about showing your true self to those closest to you, you can now rest assured that you are loved in spite of any misgivings or frailties that you allow to leak out into the world.

If you have held yourself back for fear that you might be hurt or abandoned, you can now fully immerse yourself in the experience of unconditional love.

The Queen of Hearts also gives you the strength to overcome feelings of jealousy and mistrust that work to destroy important relationships in your life.

If someone close to you has held him or herself back in any way, now is a good time to assure them there is no reason to fear abandonment.

Give those close to you the strength to fully immerse themselves in the relationship and experience the beauty of unconditional love.

QUICK REFERENCE:
You now have the opportunity to give and receive unconditional love. Rather than holding yourself back in any way, you can release fears about abandonment and feelings of jealousy. If someone close to you has held him or herself back in any way, now is a good time to assure them of your feelings. Give those close to you the strength to fully immerse themselves in the relationship and experience the beauty of unconditional love.

KING OF HEARTS

PEACE

The King of Hearts signifies a wonderful opportunity to experience peace.

Events occurring now give you the strength and opportunity to cut away the extraneous. Your external actions are in accordance with internal goals and ideals that are heartfelt to you.

You also feel a sense of serenity and understanding which gives you a greater ability to reach the goals which are most important to you.

Seek out every opportunity to gain a sense of peace. Immerse yourself in the present and work for goals and ideals which are important to you.

Peace does not have to be a fleeting sense of comfort when things go as you want them to. You can find peace in each and every moment if you strive to live your life by the values, ideals and goals that bring you your greatest sense of satisfaction and accomplishment.

Only you know what brings you peace and only you can bring peace into your life.

QUICK REFERENCE:
The King of Hearts signifies a wonderful opportunity to experience peace in your life. Peace is a state of living in accordance with your internal ideals and external circumstances, of cutting away the extraneous. Events occurring now give you the strength and opportunity to cut away the extraneous so you can live and work in accordance with external goals and internal ideals that are heartfelt for you.

CHAPTER FIVE

DIAMONDS

Diamonds are concerned with the physical world. When you pull a Diamond from the deck, there is an opportunity for improvements in your health, finances, work and home life.

♦

ACE OF DIAMONDS

NEW BEGINNING

You are receiving signals. They may be gentle nudges that drift in and out of your consciousness like a soft breeze or a sudden storm that ravages your understanding of the world and your part in it.

Your Soul is telling you that it's time to leave behind a way of life which is no longer appropriate to the person you have become.

Maybe you are unsatisfied in a relationship or unfulfilled in your job or occupation. Perhaps you want to move your home or change a habit that is working against you. Whatever the case, you are receiving signals that it's time to grow.

What's required here is a lot of inner work and contemplation. Look deep inside to understand what part of your life is no longer appropriate.

Don't make any rash decisions; try, instead, to understand everything that brought you to this crossroads. Above all else, do not fear movement. It is a sign that you are becoming stronger and wiser.

QUICK REFERENCE:
Your Inner Voice is telling you that it is time to undertake an important life change in your external world. Take time to contemplate which part of your life is no longer appropriate.

TWO OF DIAMONDS

RELEASE

You are being called to release a part of your life that is no longer appropriate to the person you have become.

Once you have undertaken this important task, you can begin building in its place a new life which is more in keeping with your needs for wholeness.

Understand that you cannot move forward until you release the part of your life that is impeding your progress.

Begin at the beginning. Picture every detail of the source of your wholeness. See it all in your mind. Take the first step now.

Remove each resistance as it arises. Don't think about what's required to get to the end of your journey or you'll be overwhelmed before you begin.

Instead, point yourself in the right direction and take each step slowly and with trust in yourself.

Remember that the change is in keeping with your deepest needs for growth.

QUICK REFERENCE:
Some part of your life is no longer appropriate to the person you have become. You must release a habit, relationship or situation which is inappropriate before you can move in more positive directions. Take one step at a time and focus on your progress, rather than how far you have left to travel.

THREE OF DIAMONDS

FEAR

When we release something in our lives and head in new directions, we often experience a sudden sense of fear. We're creatures of habit. When our habits are removed, we're left only with the unknown. The unknown can be our friend or foe. It all depends on our attitude.

If you are facing the unknown in some situation or relationship, strive to make the unknown your friend.

If you are convinced that change is needed and you are ready to undertake the work, you have nothing to fear. Saddle the unknown like you would a wild horse. Let it take you places you've always wanted to go. Let it open your eyes to the untamed potential in your nature.

If you find yourself fighting the unknown, remember: movement forward involves work and uncertainty. Growth is never an easy process. You will move forward if you release your fear and explore the unknown with an open mind.

QUICK REFERENCE:
When we release something in our lives and head in new directions, we often experience a sudden sense of fear. This is because we have removed our habits and we are left only with the unknown. Make the unknown your friend. Saddle it like you would a wild horse and let it take you places you've always wanted to go. Let it open your eyes to the untamed potential in your nature.

FOUR OF DIAMONDS

THE UNKNOWN

You may find yourself searching for signs that you are on the right path in some situation or relationship. Resist this urge.

The situation calls for you to leap into the unknown with an open mind. Close your eyes, take the first step and trust that your actions are in keeping with your needs for growth. Instead of analyzing the possible consequences and preparing yourself for success or failure, immerse yourself in the experience.

Think of the times in your past when you undertook an important change. The results you hoped for may have alluded you, yet the path ultimately led you to a new opportunity.

The Four of Diamonds gives you the strength you need to leap into the unknown, free from the burdens of expectation and anticipation.

Remember, your Soul supports movement forward and offers the encouragement of success.

QUICK REFERENCE:
You may find yourself searching for signs that you are on the right path in some situation. Resist this urge. What's required is for you to leap into the unknown with an open mind. Close your eyes, take the first step and trust that your actions are in keeping with your needs for growth.

FIVE OF DIAMONDS

MOVEMENT FORWARD

Things are speeding up in your life. New challenges and responsibilities are typical of the Five of Diamonds.

On the positive side, you are beginning to see the fruits of your labor.

People see in you a sense of meaning and understanding, and you may find that friends and family are drawn to your seemingly infectious sense of direction.

On the negative side, you may begin to grow tired of the growing number of responsibilities.

You may even have moments where you want to give up that which is demanding so much of your time and energy. Don't give up.

This is the time for movement forward and it's integral to your success that you keep forging ahead.

Stay on your current path and recognize each opening door as a wonderful and important step forward. There will be time to enjoy the results of your work later.

QUICK REFERENCE:
New challenges and responsibilities are presenting themselves now. On the positive side, you will begin seeing the fruits of your labor. On the negative side, you may have moments when you want to give up the challenges and responsibilities which are demanding so much of your energy and time. It is integral to your success that you keep forging ahead.

SIX OF DIAMONDS

PROSPERITY -- SUCCESS

You have come full circle in your efforts to improve your external world. You've identified a need for change, accomplished the work and now you can rest assured all your efforts were not in vain.

This card signifies a wonderful advancement in some part of your outer world: career, finances, health, the completion of a project, reaching a personal goal or perhaps improving a relationship that was in need of repair.

If you are just starting to see the results of your efforts, keep laying the ground work. If you are already tasting the sweet fruits of your labor, enjoy and rejuvenate.

The only threat here is in losing your humility. Remain humble and share your good fortune. Try also to remember the fulfillment that comes from overcoming obstacles. That way, the next time you are presented with a challenge -- and there will always be another challenge -- the hill will be much easier to climb.

QUICK REFERENCE:
This card signifies wonderful advancement in some part of your outer world -- perhaps a career advancement, financial gain, improved health or the completion of some project which is important to you. Enjoy your good fortune, but don't forget your humility. If you remain humble and grateful, your success will have deep and lasting meaning.

SEVEN OF DIAMONDS

OVER EXTENSION

Patterns of over extension are at the forefront of some part of your external life. You are failing to recognize your physical limits and boundaries.

Is someone else making you work beyond your limits or are *you* jeopardizing your physical health and well-being?

It's always up to you to recognize when you've pushed yourself too far. If you feel worn out or taken advantage of in some situation or relationship, honor your limits. Take time for yourself. Eat well, rest, exercise and restore your physical balance.

Remember the difference between quality and quantity. When you operate beyond your limits, the quality of your work suffers. Rather than enjoying the results of all your hard work, you will be disappointed that your extra effort has resulted in a mediocre product.

When you approach your work with bright eyes and a well-rested Soul, you will discover and harness your greatest potential.

QUICK REFERENCE:
You are being pushed beyond your physical and emotional boundaries. Seek to discover if someone else is pushing you beyond your limits or if *you* are jeopardizing your own well-being. It's always up to you to recognize when you are operating beyond your limits.

EIGHT OF DIAMONDS

CROSSROADS

You may find a difficult decision lies ahead. You've achieved some external success on your current path and you've grown as a result. You've enjoyed the road on which you've traveled, but perhaps it is becoming all too familiar and predictable.

Now you may be thinking of heading in a new direction and leaving all your familiar surroundings behind. This may be a difficult time for you. There are potential benefits and sacrifices regardless of which path you choose.

The easiest path might be the one you are on because you understand the terrain. Yet, if you are on the wrong path, the most difficult thing may be hanging on.

Look for signs from within. Your inner voice will help you decide which road is best.

Remember, the most difficult part of the journey is deciding which path to take. From there, simply put one foot in front of the other until you reach your destination.

QUICK REFERENCE:
You may be facing a crossroads in some situation or relationship. You've achieved some external success on your current path, but may be finding that your place in the world is becoming familiar and predictable. Look for signs from within. Your inner voice is a patient and useful guide. Remember, the most difficult part of the journey is in deciding which route to take.

NINE OF DIAMONDS

DEFINING SUCCESS

This card is concerned with defining your deepest needs for success.

Do you require material possessions and financial security or are you led by less tangible ideals such as self rule, creative expression or intellectual development?

Do you find your greatest joy in the company of close friends and family or are you more at home among corporate colleagues?

Contemplate what makes you happy and fulfilled from the deepest core of who you are. Ask yourself if your external actions are in keeping with your definition of success.

If the answer is no, try to put more time and effort into reaching goals which are in alignment with your needs for happiness and fulfillment.

Too many people toil in unsatisfying jobs and look to weekends and holidays as their time to live when, with effort and dedication, they could find ways of successfully living every moment of their lives.

QUICK REFERENCE:
This card is concerned with defining your deepest needs for success. Do you require material possessions and financial security or are you led by less tangible ideals such as self rule, creative expression or intellectual development? Contemplate what makes you happy from the deepest core of who you are. Ask yourself if your external actions are in keeping with your definition of success.

TEN OF DIAMONDS

WHOLENESS

You have come to yourself in some aspect of your external world. You have defined your needs for success and you can now take great strides forward in reaching the external goals which are most important to you.

Whether involving your health, finances, possessions or your home, you can find lasting external wholeness if you stay on your present course and continually maintain your aim toward your physical goals.

Remember, however, that success in your physical world does not automatically bring happiness and fulfillment.

You must also nourish the other parts of your nature: your mind, spirit and emotions.

External success alone brings only emptiness. External success, combined with mental challenges, spiritual insight and strong emotional relationships, is the true definition of success.

Strive to bring wholeness to all arenas of your life and you will be truly blessed.

QUICK REFERENCE:
You have come to yourself in some part of your external world. You have defined your needs for success and you can now take great strides forward in reaching physical goals which are important to you (whether involving your health, finances, possessions or your home). Remember, however, that success in your physical world does not automatically bring happiness and fulfillment. You must also nourish the other parts of your nature: your mind, spirit and emotions.

JACK OF DIAMONDS

THE PRESENT

What's called for here is to maintain a constant, steady pace and live for the present.

If you can find fulfillment, joy and satisfaction in the doing -- rather than the receiving -- you will always be whole.

Many of us live in a perpetual state of waiting: "I'll be happy when..." or "Things will be better when...." If you find yourself focused on results and looking for fulfillment in the destination, rather than the journey, try to remember the precarious nature of life.

If your life were to end tomorrow, could your loved ones say you led a full life and enjoyed the time you had or would they be left with the tragic knowledge that you sacrificed your happiness in the present for goals which would never be?

Don't stop working for your goals. Don't just look to your goals as your source of happiness. Instead, look for happiness, wholeness and satisfaction in the smallest of life's blessings.

QUICK REFERENCE:
Live for the present, this card is saying. If you find yourself focused on results and looking for fulfillment in the destination, rather than the journey, try to remember the precarious nature of life. If your life were to end tomorrow, could your loved ones say you led a full life and enjoyed the time you had or would they be left with the tragic knowledge that you sacrificed your happiness in the present for goals which would never be?

QUEEN OF DIAMONDS

PAUSE -- REFLECT

You may be unclear of how to act in a certain situation or relationship. It may seem as though some event has come to its conclusion and yet there is still work to be done.

What's required here is closure. Before you can put an end to a certain situation or event, you must find meaning.

Pause, be still and reflect. Try to understand why this event took place and what you learned as a result.

Think about how this event influenced your character, your relationships, your beliefs about the world and your understanding of your self.

Discover the ways in which you've grown and become stronger.

Once you fully understand why this event presented itself, you can incorporate your new-found understanding into all parts of your life.

You will know you have learned all you can from this event when you find yourself facing a new challenge and a new opportunity to grow.

QUICK REFERENCE:
You may be unclear how to act in some situation or relationship. It may seem as though some situation has come to its final conclusion and yet there is still work to be done. What's required here is closure. Try to understand why this event took place and what you learned as a result. Think about how this event influenced your character, your relationships, your beliefs about the world and your understanding of yourself.

KING OF DIAMONDS

DEATH

There is a successful conclusion to some situation, event or relationship. All the energy that has been devoted to trying to bring about positive change can now be released.

Rest and restore your energy. Enjoy what you have gained -- whether it be a material reward, spiritual growth, mental development or emotional fulfillment.

Soon you will be asked to undertake the next challenge required in the evolution of your Soul.

Keep in mind what you have gained from this recent challenge. Remember that the sacrifices and hardships were well worth the resulting growth and development.

This knowledge will give you added strength and understanding when you encounter the next challenge.

While there may be reason to celebrate your advancement, strive to remain humble. Humility in successes and failures will bring balance into all parts of your life.

QUICK REFERENCE:
There is a successful conclusion to some situation, event or relationship. All the energy that has been devoted to trying to bring about positive change can now be released. Rest and restore. Soon you will be asked to undertake the next challenge required in the evolution of your Soul. The only advice here is this: remain humble.

CHAPTER SIX

CLUBS

Clubs are concerned with spiritual energy.
When you pull a Club from the deck, there is an
opportunity for a strengthened sense of
intuition, understanding and
spiritual evolution.

*The Clubs are based on Carl Jung's
Archetypes of the Collective Unconscious.
These are personality traits we all share.*

ACE OF CLUBS

SHADOW

You may be having trouble getting in touch with your Shadow. Your Shadow is the dark and often repressed side of your nature, the place where you bury feelings of selfishness, anger, resentment, jealousy, fear and greed.

Your Shadow comes to the forefront when you lose control of your emotions and find yourself saying or doing things that you later regret.

The Shadow is very much a part of your nature. The more you try to bury and deny your Shadow, the more it struggles to bring to the surface all the negative feelings and impulses which need to be expressed and released. Strive to release your darker emotions as they emerge.

If you hold them back, you allow them to grow in strength and negatively influence your life.

If you understand them as a valid part of who you are, they are less likely to erupt inappropriately and do harm to your life and your relationships.

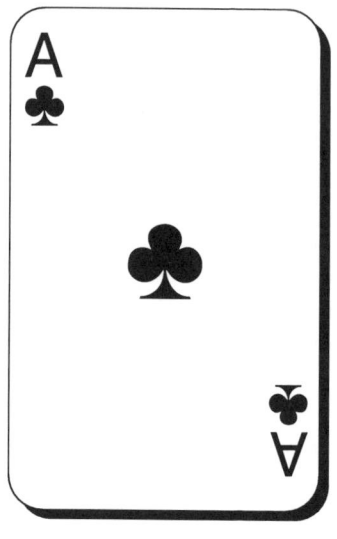

QUICK REFERENCE:
You may be having trouble getting in touch with your Shadow. This is the dark and often repressed side of your nature, the place where you bury feelings of selfishness, anger, resentment, jealousy, fear and greed. The Shadow is very much a part of your nature. Strive to release your darker emotions as they emerge.

TWO OF CLUBS

PERSONA

Each one of us wears many hats in our lives: the nurturing parent, the responsible provider, the reliable employee, the attentive spouse, the law-abiding citizen. Some are given to us by society, and others are created by ourselves as a means of feeling valuable and being accepted.

Personas can serve a negative and a positive function. At best, they help society function in an orderly and productive fashion. At worst, they can limit an individual's understanding of him or herself to a superficial level.

When you pull this card, it may mean that you are limiting your understanding of yourself. You may be seeing yourself at a superficial level, rather than exploring all sides of your nature.

It is important to live up to your many responsibilities to family, friends, employers and society. But this is not all that you are. The responsible provider can still explore the playful child within.

QUICK REFERENCE:
The Two of Clubs urges you not to limit your understanding of yourself to a superficial level. You wear many hats in your life: the responsible provider, the reliable employee, the law-abiding citizen...but this is not all that you are. It is important to live up to your many responsibilities, but the provider can still explore the playful child within.

THREE OF CLUBS

ANIMA

The Anima is the "traditionally" feminine side of your nature: the nurturing, patient, sensitive side of the personality found in men and women.

When the Three of Clubs is drawn, it may be an indication that you have fallen out of balance and become too focused on the sensitive, nurturing side of your nature.

You may find that you are easily upset or quickly wounded by words or reactions which are not meant to hurt you.

You may find that you are too focused on taking care of others needs and ignoring your own needs in a certain situation or relationship.

Explore why your Anima has come to the forefront. Once you understand why you have become overly sensitive, or focused on others needs at the expense of your own needs, you can strive to regain balance and approach situations with the benefit of both the feminine and masculine sides of your nature.

QUICK REFERENCE:
You are not operating in balance. Your Anima, the "traditionally" feminine side of your nature, is at the forefront causing you to feel overly sensitive, easily hurt or focused on taking care of others' needs at the expense of your own. Explore why your Anima has come to the forefront. Once you understand why you have fallen out of balance, you can strive to regain the use of both the feminine and masculine sides of your nature.

FOUR OF CLUBS

ANIMUS

The opposite of the Anima (the feminine side of your nature) is the Animus. This is the aggressive, logical, results-oriented part of the personality that is "traditionally" associated with men, but found in both men and women.

When the Four of Clubs is drawn, it may be an indication that you have fallen out of balance and become too focused on the Animus in your nature.

You may find you are forgetting others' feelings and ignoring the "human factor" in some situation or relationship. You may be so focused on results, success and advancement that you are forgetting to look for your own emotional fulfillment or you are forgetting the emotional needs of others.

Explore why your Animus has come to the forefront. Once you understand why you have fallen out of balance, you can strive to approach situations and relationships with the benefit of both the feminine and masculine sides of your nature.

QUICK REFERENCE:
The Animus is the opposite of the Anima. It is the aggressive, logical, results-oriented side in your nature. This card is telling you that you may have fallen out of balance and become too focused on advancement and results at the expense of your emotional needs or the emotional needs of others. Strive to regain balance and approach situations and relationships with the benefit of both the feminine and masculine sides of your nature.

FIVE OF CLUBS

SELF

The Five of Clubs is a wonderful card, signifying your direct contact with the spiritual forces in your nature.

The Self allows you to utilize your magical gifts in ways that can bring about positive change in your life and the lives of those close to you.

Listen to your intuition and take note of any synchronistic events that are beginning to appear in your life. Strive to understand the messages you receive and act on the direction you are given.

Often, when the Self is involved, you will find that those around you, sometimes even strangers, offer advice which can improve your life and the lives of those close to you.

You'll find that your psychic gifts -- while always present -- are clear and readily available for use in bringing about positive change.

There is one reminder: this time of heightened clarity will not last forever. Make use of this insight in positive and constructive ways.

QUICK REFERENCE:
The Five of Clubs signifies your direct contact with the spiritual forces in your nature. There is a heightened ability to use your magical gifts in ways that bring about positive change in your life and the lives of those close to you.

SIX OF CLUBS

MOTHER

The Mother represents your infinite capacity to nurture, give love and compassion.

You may find yourself offering or being asked to nurture others. You have the wonderful ability to say exactly what those around you need to hear and do things that make others feel happier and more at ease.

There are three warnings associated with this card.

The first is that you may become focused on others' needs at the expense of your own needs.

The second warning is that in comforting others and suggesting paths they should take, you may unintentionally influence them to choose a path that benefits you more than them.

The final warning is that in "helping" others, you may inadvertently take away their control. Don't be an overbearing mother or you'll end up with a dependent child. When those around you ask for support, understand that they aren't giving you control.

QUICK REFERENCE:
The Mother card is communicating your infinite ability to nurture and give love to those around you. Remember to use it wisely. If someone comes to you for compassion, don't offer them solutions or take away their control of the situation. Instead, support them in their decisions.

SEVEN OF CLUBS

FATHER

When you receive the Seven of Clubs, you may be functioning as a Father to those close to you. You have new-found strength to protect others from harm and provide for their needs.

People are drawn to you because they feel safe and secure. They see you as a responsible parent who can assist them in overcoming obstacles in their lives.

The positive side of this card is that you have the ability to assist and help people who are currently lacking the strength to help themselves.

The danger is that while you try to assist and aid those around you, you may also be over-protecting them.

Remember, sometimes people need to experience discomfort or uncertainty in order to grow. Some lessons are not easily learned.

If you shelter them from the sometimes messy experiences of life, you are depriving them of experiences which could lead to growth and fulfillment.

QUICK REFERENCE:
The Father is operating at the center of your nature. This is the part of your personality which strives to protect, shelter and provide for those around you. People are drawn to you because they feel safe. However, take pains not to be over-protective, or you could prevent those closest to you from experiencing situations which are integral to their growth and development.

EIGHT OF CLUBS

DIVINE CHILD

This is the part of your personality that has a great ability to re-discover the child within. You find yourself feeling uninhibited and wanting to play. You see a new sense of wonder, excitement and pleasure in the world. You are able to release the burdens of adulthood, put aside anxiety about reaching goals and shrug off fears about consequences.

If you have been too focused on goals, responsibilities and the burdens of adulthood, this card is telling you to lighten up, enjoy yourself and take part in some of the amusements that life has to offer.

If you feel you cannot relax and enjoy yourself until a difficult situation is resolved, this card is telling you that your answer may also lie in your ability to see the situation through the eyes of a child.

The Divine Child inside can assist you in seeing all situations at their purest and most simple level. This is where you will find truth which is free of clutter and pretence.

QUICK REFERENCE:
The Divine Child stands for your ability to re-discover the wonder, excitement and playfulness in your nature. If you have been too focused on the burdens of adulthood, this card is telling you to lighten up and enjoy yourself. If you feel you cannot enjoy yourself until a difficult situation is resolved, this card is telling you that your answer may also lie in your ability to see the situation through the eyes of a child.

NINE OF CLUBS

MAIDEN

Traditionally the Maiden was the mediator between two opposites: good and evil; heaven and hell; light and dark. She was given the difficult job of bringing opposing forces together for the betterment of the community.

If you find yourself acting as a mediator between two people, strive to bring about a compromise. Perhaps you can incorporate the strengths from both forces to create a stronger whole or you can use the strengths of one side to counter the weaknesses of the other.

If you are faced with a choice between two alternate paths, try to find a compromise.

First you must find the stillness necessary to distinguish between your outward wants and the inner wisdom of your Soul. Then, it is simply a matter of accomplishing the work.

As in all journeys, the most difficult part is in uncovering the correct path. From there, just put one foot in front of the other until you reach your destiny.

QUICK REFERENCE:
Traditionally, the Maiden was the mediator between light and dark; heaven and hell; good and evil. You may be asked to act as a mediator between two people or choose between two alternate paths. First, find the stillness to distinguish between your outward wants and the inner wisdom of your soul. Then act as the mediator and find a way to reach a compromise.

TEN OF CLUBS

HERO

Comic books and movies depict the hero as a strong, courageous and generous individual. The Ten of Clubs is telling you that you have these exceptional qualities and can use them to improve your life and the lives of those around you.

If you are looking for solutions to a troubling situation in your own life, look within and discover the Hero in your Soul.

If you encounter others, even strangers, who are confused or troubled in any arena of their lives, act as the Hero and selflessly offer your assistance.

The Hero does not look for recognition or praise. The Hero reacts in a selfless and helping manner, placing humanity above personal gain.

Acts of heroism can be as grand as saving a life or as subtle as slowing down for a merging motorist.

Even the smallest act of kindness sends a gentle challenge into the sea of humanity -- one which can carry far beyond view.

QUICK REFERENCE:
The Hero signifies that you have the exceptional qualities of strength, courage and generosity and can use them to improve your life and the lives of those around you. If you are looking for solutions to a troubling situation in your own life, look within and discover the Hero in your Soul. If you encounter others, even strangers, who are confused or troubled, act as the Hero and selflessly offer your assistance.

JACK OF CLUBS

WISE OLD MAN

Every now and then, each one of us is struck with an awesome and magical moment of clarity. Suddenly, we find ourselves with a crystal-clear understanding of the meaning of our lives and the workings of the universe.

As if hit by lightening, our world seemingly turns upside down and all the answers we've ever hoped for are suddenly ours for the taking.

You have reached this level of clarity in some situation or relationship. Like the Wise Old Man who sits in solitude and contemplates his thoughts and ideas, you may find that you are compelled to remove yourself from daily life to explore the depth of the knowledge and understanding that is now open to you.

Don't be afraid to retreat. Take full advantage of the moment. You will find the Wise Old Man in your Soul will not only give you answers, but also a new-found sense of inspiration, energy and profound happiness.

QUICK REFERENCE:
The Wise Old Man is working in your nature. You receive almost magical clarity on issues that previously left you puzzled. You may also find that you want to retreat to explore the depth of the knowledge and understanding that is now open to you. Don't be afraid to retreat. You will find a new-found sense of inspiration, energy and happiness.

QUEEN OF CLUBS

TRICKSTER

When an individual attains wisdom (Wise Old Man), he must first retreat and contemplate his new-found knowledge. Then, once he has grown comfortable with these ideas, he again looks outward and incorporates this knowledge into his life. He becomes the Trickster.

You are operating as the Trickster. You have attained the highest level of knowledge and wisdom. Having incorporated this clarity into your life, you have freed yourself from all the petty and unimportant worries of life.

You find a new sense of playfulness and fun. You don't get dragged down by setbacks or inconveniences. Why get dragged down by unimportant details when life is a wonderful, magical -- and, above all, fleeting -- opportunity to laugh, love and play?

Instead of cursing traffic jams, you can easily find pleasure in every moment you have on this earth. Laugh and remind others to live well.

QUICK REFERENCE:
You have become the Trickster. You have attained the highest level of wisdom and now you can take advantage of every moment you have on this earth. You are no longer dragged down by petty problems or setbacks. Instead, you recognize life as a fleeting opportunity to laugh, love and play.

KING OF CLUBS

CONJUNCTIO (UNION)

When two people who love and respect each other join, each becomes a better individual. Together, they become a perfect whole.

You are in the process of combining two individual elements (whether they be your work and home life, an interest and a skill, beliefs and actions or the actual joining of two people) to create a better whole.

If you are uncertain about combining two elements in your life, know that this card supports success and fulfillment.

You will soon experience the positive results of this joining, whether they be material gain, spiritual growth, mental development or emotional fulfillment.

There is one gentle reminder when the joining of two people is involved: strive to retain your sense of self. A relationship between two separate and whole individuals, who join in love and retain their independence, is Conjunctio (the perfect union).

QUICK REFERENCE:
Success is assured in the joining of two people, two situations, two ideas or two relationships to create two stronger individual elements and one greater whole. If the joining of two people is involved, strive to retain your uniqueness and independence and you will know the perfect union.

Belinda Atkinson was born in Kelowna, British Columbia, Canada, in 1966. From early childhood, she had a fascination with Divination, Parapsychology and the Paranormal and fostered her interest through books, movies and experimentation.

Belinda graduated from the Journalism Arts program at Calgary's Southern Alberta Institute of Technology in 1986 and went on to work as a news reporter, feature writer, business reporter and education reporter at a number of community newspapers in Alberta and British Columbia while, in her spare time, she became an avid reader of Runes, I-Ching and numerous methods of Tarot. In her experimentation, she came to the conclusion that answers in readings come not from outside or occult forces, but directly from within. They are the Soul's way of reaching out to the consciousness and helping people to understand the internal and external influences in their past, present and future.

Belinda became tired of using Tarot cards and, in 1992, turned her attention to playing cards as a preferred method of Divination. She found that the interpretations available were often negative and left the subject of a reading feeling as though they had no control in changing or improving situations in their lives. She set out to create an interpretation that would be positive, healing, motivational, easy to understand and accessible to anyone with a regular deck of cards.

Her first published book, *Tarot of the Soul,* is the result.

NOTES

NOTES

NOTES

NOTES

NOTES